ERIC HOUGHTON

The MAGIC Cheese

illustrated by
CHARLES FUGE

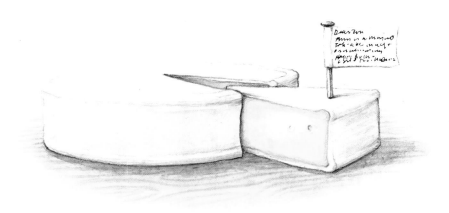

LONDON
VICTOR GOLLANCZ LTD
1991

First published in Great Britain 1991
by Victor Gollancz Ltd
14 Henrietta Street, London WC2E 8QJ

Text © Eric Houghton 1991
Illustrations © Charles Fuge 1991

British Library Cataloguing in Publication Data
Houghton, Eric
The magic cheese.
I. Title   II. Fuge, Charles
823'.914 [J]

ISBN 0-575-04896-4

Printed in Singapore by Imago Publishing Ltd

On Tom's birthday, his uncle sent him a cheese.
It had a note stuck on top, like a flag.

Dear Tom,
This is a magic cheese.
Take a bite before going to sleep,
and it will give you special dreams.
Happy Birthday!
Love from Uncle Ebenezer

Tom had a wonderful birthday. And when bedtime
came, he remembered to eat a bit of the magic cheese.

Uncle Ebenezer was right. The cheese gave him a special
dream about a Bogglepuss. The Bogglepuss was covered with
orange stripes and blue blobs, and it lived in the jungle. It put
Tom on its back and galumphed through the trees, making
monkeys leap and parrots screech.

When Tom woke in the morning, he found how magic the cheese really was, for there was his dream come to life, sitting on his bed.

"That's the best ride I've ever had!" said Tom.

The Bogglepuss purred. Then it hopped off the bed, lumbered over the carpet and curled up next to the wardrobe.

Tom was delighted. Everything the Bogglepuss touched became covered with orange stripes and blue blobs, just like the Bogglepuss.

Tom hoped his mother wouldn't mind. He went downstairs to breakfast.

When Tom came to bed that evening, he found that the Bogglepuss
had been wandering around, looking for cosier places to curl up in.
Several more things had blue blobs and orange stripes. The
Bogglepuss was now snuggled down in Tom's bed.

Tom decided to sleep on the carpet. As he lay down, he ate
more of the magic cheese. Perhaps he could dream the
Bogglepuss back into its jungle.

The cheese gave him another marvellous dream. It was about a
Wongler. The Wongler was fat and lived under the sea. Tom
climbed on its back, and it swam down below the waves.

They chased rainbow fish and sang songs with huge whales.
They played hide-and-seek in coral caves and explored seaweed
forests, where sea-horses pranced and starfish twinkled.

When Tom awoke, he found the cheese had worked again, for there was the Wongler sitting on his bed.

"That's the best swim I've ever had," said Tom.

The Wongler crawled around the room, sniffing here and sniffing there, before snuggling down by the chest of drawers.

Tom was fascinated. Everything the Wongler sniffed grew fatter and fatter, until it was as plump as the Wongler.

Tom hoped his mother wouldn't mind. He went downstairs to breakfast.

When Tom came to bed that night, he found that the Bogglepuss and the Wongler had been wandering about, touching and sniffing. Now they were both tucked up in bed, snoring.

Tom ate another piece of the magic cheese, and settled down to sleep on the carpet. Now he had two animals to dream away.

The cheese gave him another wonderful dream. It was about a Flutterlump. The Flutterlump was a big bird, as light as a balloon. Tom scrambled on its back, and it took a deep breath and floated up into the air.

Higher and higher they rose — over trees, over towns, over mountains. Still they climbed — till they reached the fleecy, floating clouds.

Tom gasped with delight as the buoyant Flutterlump soared this way and that, zooming among cotton-wool cliffs and caverns.

When Tom awoke, the Flutterlump was on the bed, preening its feathers.

"You flew like a jet fighter!" gasped Tom.

The Flutterlump blinked modestly, then floated around the room, poking its beak into likely nesting-places.

Finally it came to roost on top of the wardrobe.

Tom was entranced. Everything the Flutterlump's beak touched became lighter than air and floated upwards, just like the Flutterlump had done.

Tom hoped his mother wouldn't mind. He went downstairs to breakfast.

That evening, Tom found the Bogglepuss, the Wongler and the Flutterlump packed tight in his bed, fast asleep. As he settled down on the carpet, he realised he would have to do something drastic. There should be some way to send the dreams back: perhaps by eating twice as much cheese...

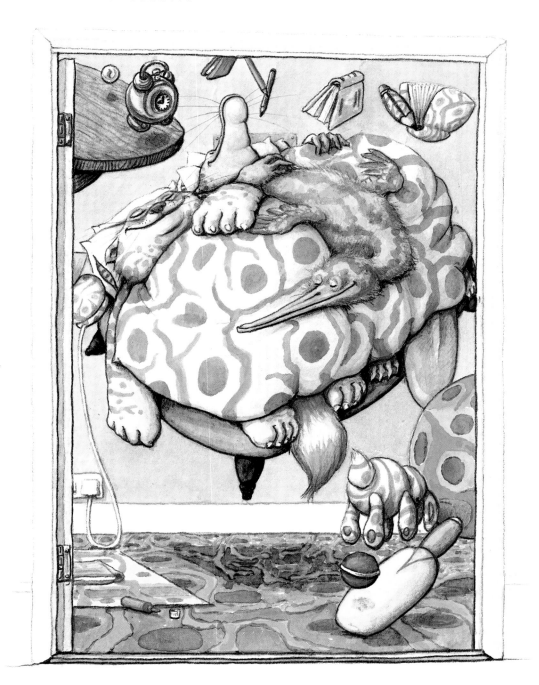

He had a nightmare. It was about a Grakkensplott. The Grakkensplott had a hundred teeth and sharp claws. It wanted him for supper.

Tom ran as hard as he could — but the Grakkensplott ran faster still, licking its lips and waving its spiky tail.

Suddenly Tom tripped and fell. The Grakkensplott pounced, opening its jaws wide. Tom glimpsed rows of fierce, frightening teeth —

Then he woke up. He was trembling. Thankfully he realised it had only been a dream. He was safe in his own room.

Or was he?

He looked up.

There was the Grakkensplott — grinning at him with teeth like white needles. The Bogglepuss, the Wongler and the Flutterlump were sitting up in bed, dumbfounded.

Tom shook with fear.

The Grakkensplott crept closer. Its tail rasped against the wardrobe and its jaws began to open...

And then —

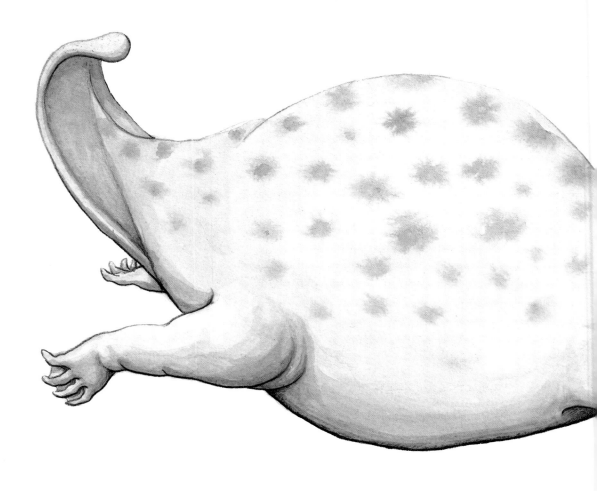

All at once the Bogglepuss snarled, the Wongler screeched, and the Flutterlump squawked. They hurled themselves out of bed and on top of the startled Grakkensplott!

Tails thrashed, teeth gnashed, claws clashed. Shrieks and
squeals shook the room, as the four animals whirled and
struggled and tumbled in one huge tangled ball...
    Then all went quiet.
    Fearfully Tom opened his eyes.

He couldn't believe what he saw. Swollen enormously fat, and looking ridiculous in orange stripes and blue blobs, the Grakkensplott was floating helplessly against the ceiling.

The Bogglepuss, the Wongler and the Flutterlump dusted each other off, looking pleased with themselves. Then, taking a deep breath, the Flutterlump floated up to the ceiling. It took careful aim with its beak and punctured the plump Grakkensplott just like bursting a balloon.

BANG! And the Grakkensplott had gone.

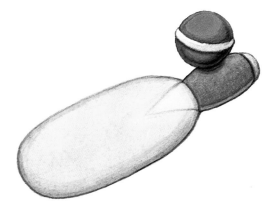

Tom bounced on the bed with delight.
   "You saved me!" he cried. Then he added thoughtfully,
"There must be a really good way of thanking you..."

The three dream-animals looked at each other, nodding vigorously. Then they turned the magic cheese upside down, and eagerly held it up for Tom to see.

Tom looked. On the bottom of it, Uncle Ebenezer had written:

> To return the dreams,
> eat some cheese and count
> backwards from a hundred.

So Tom did — after many sad and loving goodbyes.

When he woke next morning,
everything in his room was back to
normal — and the dream-animals
had gone. In fact there was
absolutely no trace that he'd ever
had three such wonderful, kind
and brave friends.

Except for one thing...

To Tom—
with love